The Whispering Flower

By: Jasmine Garrison

Special Thanks

To everyone who believed in me and helped to make
this possible. I am forever grateful.

~I Love You~

PROLOGUE

All Skie could remember were the doo-wop songs of the late 50s that played on repeat in the car before her life changed for the "worst." As her dad beat the steering wheel like a drum and her mom harmonized with Skie, thoughts of anything going wrong were highly unthinkable. Everything was perfect.

As they crossed the intersection, an alteration in the atmosphere made it's way into their lives, traumatizing Skie forever. A forever horrifying incident was seen through the eyes of many, giving them courage and a sense of urgency to call for help.

The screeches, the screams seemed to have slowed down, as well as the four tires that flew everywhere around them. The sounds of arriving ambulances and police cars surrounded them, but the

noise was muffled. The tragedy was unbelievable and
unthinkable. How could the most perfect day flip on
its back and show us its worst?

CHAPTER ONE

As if it was on a personal mission to destroy, the huge back of the 18 wheeler slammed right into the car sending Skie to the opposite window, which stirred up panic and confusion. She could see her unconscious parents, lying there as emergency responders came forth to help. Shaken with panic, Skie didn't even want to be touched. This was so unbelievable.

Skie and her parents were all put into separate emergency trucks and sent to the nearest hospital where emergency doctors and nurses awaited their arrival to take immediate action.

Each of them were assigned to different rooms, with Skie being the last one in. She still felt dizzy and unaware of anything even though she knew where she was and what had happened. Exhausted in pain and panic, Skie eventually loses consciousness.

~~~

A few hours later, around 5pm, Skie awakened in a room, alone with monitors and wires plugged in around her sounding unfamiliar tunes. Skie was panicked and desperate to find her parents. With determination, she got out of bed and removed the wires attached to her and went on a mission to find her mother.

"Skie what are you doing here?" her mother asked in a soft whisper as she lay still bearing the pain of her injuries yet trying to show strength.

"I wanted to see you and talk to you. I need you to tell me your favorite saying again." Skie replied, teary-eyed.

"Nobody can hurt you more than this world, baby. Don't you ever forget that. Don't you ever forget that I love you either."

"I'll never forget it momma."

"Do you promise?"

"Yes I promise."

"That's my girl. I love you."

"I love you, too."

A bit too soon, her mother closed her eyes and took her last breath right in front of Skie as the alarms from the monitoring equipment grew louder and nurses and doctors rushed in.

Skie knew, that she couldn't cry. She saw it coming and there was no point in crying if she knew that her mother was in Heaven.

Later on, when she went to visit her dad. The famous last words of her mother were told by her father as well. And like dominoes slowly falling in her family, he repeated the same behavior as the last and closed his eyes before taking in his last breath to paradise.

Returning to her own hospital room unnoticed, Skie realized that her life would never again be the same.

CHAPTER TWO

Skie woke up to the chirping of birds outside her window and found herself talking to her whispering flower. It told her encouraging things like how pretty she was, and it cured all her insecurities. Today it did not reply, and Skie got a little upset and made her way to the kitchen.

She poured herself some apple cider and sat down at the kitchen table and studied the bubbles in her drink. As each bubble rose, the air on top of it stopped it from rising any further, causing her to sigh helplessly. The disappearing of each bubble reminded her of her parents.

Ever since she was 17, Skie has been living in the house given to her by her parents, alone. Both her parents died in a tragic car accident. Skie could've died too, but through some miracle of God, she survived, except for her limbs being broken. They soon healed.

She watched both her parents take their last breaths calmly, her mother being first. The last words from her father were "I love you" and the thought of those last words brought her to tears.

~~~

The night after her parents died, Skie's Aunt Alicia decided to visit. As she knocked on the door, knowing Skie would not be expecting anyone, she hoped and prayed that she would be welcomed. Skie immediately took in the comfort of her aunt.

Every night that Skie was there, Aunt Alicia told stories about her parents even though she knew Skie was depressed, but she also knew that she could use the company. Skie was told that in high school, her parents were just friends and her aunt was the one that fell in love with Skie's father. Her mother found him a nuisance.

One day Skie's father came to the house and asked for her mother instead of Aunt Alicia, which made her mad. It turns out that Skie's mother actually did have feelings for him even though she called him a nuisance. Her aunt called it scandalous, but her mother called it love.

After that, Skie's parents became closer than ever and eventually her aunt got over the heartbreak. And now, there was no way she could hold it against her own sister. She said that it is never right to be mad at someone you won't ever be able to see again.

On the last day of her aunt's visit, they talked about the whispering flower which her aunt found very interesting and extraordinary. Skie told her the story on how it was found:

One day Skie decided that she needed to go for a walk to clear her mind of the overwhelming sensation of the fact that her parents had just died. As she walked past her Grandmother's house, which was down the road, she stumbled over a dying flower in the cracks of the sidewalks. It was whimpering, sighing, begging for water. That's when she carefully took it up and planted it in an old vase her mother used just for decoration. Ever since then, the flower repaid her with compliments and encouragement.

After hearing the story, her Aunt Alicia was even more fascinated at what the flower was capable of and wanted to get a compliment from it. Her aunt asked Skie if she could have a moment with the flower alone. Skie allowed it and made her way into the kitchen, but before Skie could even close the kitchen door, her aunt began pouring out questions to the flower. Skie laughed to herself, closed the door, and stood close to eavesdrop.

In the kitchen, Skie could hear the conversation, partially. She tried to make out the muffled sentences that fell out her aunt's mouth and the whispers that came out of the flower. Of course, she would not be able to hear the whispers of her flower, but she did hear a bit of what her aunt said.

"...want to meet her. You should tell her I love her." her aunt said, as Skie leaned her ear a bit closer to the door of the kitchen. "She's an amazing...don't know what she's doing now...she has my heart." Skie smiled to herself as she realized her aunt had been talking about her. *If she wanted to know what I'd been up to, then why not ask?* Skie thought.

Skie decided to come out of the kitchen and when she did, her aunt just looked at her and smiled. "I should go pack up." Skie nodded and let her aunt go on her way. She walked up to the whispering flower and asked, "What did she tell you?" The flower whispered back, "She loves you and don't ever forget that."

"My aunt right?"

The flower fell silent and her aunt came back in the room with her stuff in the same suitcases that she had when she walked in a week ago. Skie gave her a kiss at the door and watched as she drove away and vanished into the darkness of the night.

CHAPTER THREE

The day after her aunt left Skie to be on her own, she realized that family was not what she needed to feel better about herself or the incident. She walked up to her whispering flower and said good morning. It had talked to both her and Aunt Alicia for the past week.

Except for today.

It was quiet today. Maybe it was the dawning of a new problem in the world. Maybe it was some mistake she had made. Was it a premonition of something to come? Was that something good or bad? She could only find out later if her flower wasn't saying anything. She forgot about it and just continued on with the day.

Skie decided just to begin her normal morning walk and try the flower later. She hasn't been in school since her parents' deaths and now that she's 19, there seems to be no point for it - unless she can just skip through college.

As she opened the old screen door to walk outside, it screeched and reminded her of the screams that filled the car during the accident that sent both her parents to paradise.

She stifled in some tears and then let out a large breath of air. As she made her way to the corner she listened to the birds sing and watched as a dove fluttered above her head, reminding her of her angels. A smile made its way to her face and she didn't bother to wipe it off.

The neighborhood was quiet today. Cars passed, but nobody honked horns. People stood on sidewalks, but their voices were quiet. They all had a smile on their face as if something amazing was to happen today. If there was a meaning for happiness, this would be it. Sadly, Skie didn't feel that way. She felt as if the start of the day was okay, but it will only get worse from here.

That's when the words of her mother clicked in her head: *Nobody can hurt you more than this world, baby.* Now 19, instead of being a young kid when she was first told the saying, she understands the meaning. No one person can hurt you more than the crime and disease in the world. Mankind is always in a daily battle between good and evil. There is a constant battle between those that are of good and those that are of the darkness and wickedness of the world. In Skie's mind, it is that same spirit of wickedness that took her parents away and left her on Earth to deal with it.

As she turned the corner, she passed two two men dressed in ragged clothing with suspicious eyes and shady smiles at the end of the road. She could hear them babbling on about gambling, money, and other unimportant matters of street life.

Skie's neighborhood wasn't the richest or the poorest in the city. It was an interesting mixture of people: old, young, not so rich, not so poor, hard workers, not so hard workers, big criminals, small criminals. Skie's parents were excellent examples of the hard working element in the neighborhood. Her dad, a local business man, always wore nicely ironed jeans with a shirt and bowtie. Her mom, an elementary school counselor, always wore her hair pinned up tight and vintage style dresses, which was common for the ladies in the neighborhood. On the other hand, those in the neighborhood who were less interested in hard work or keeping the community a safe place were easily recognized in their ragged, oversized, dark, unkempt clothing style.

As Skie passed the two men, something told her to go home when she suddenly realized she had made a wrong turn. She was too dazed to even quickly locate an escape route when she saw *them*. They were the only gang in town. They were known for carrying weapons and causing chaos. They came around the corner parallel to Skie with their guns drawn to the sky. Skie ran as fast as she could in the opposite direction towards the woods.

Gunshots rang in her ears, tearing her eardrums apart. She made it halfway through the woods before stopping to catch her breath. She could still hear the gunshots which meant that she hadn't made it far enough in. She said a quick prayer as she layed on the ground, face in the dirt. Mosquitos and birds flew past her like she wasn't even there. When she got back up, everything was quiet and the sun had gone down. It seemed like she'd been praying for dear life for only 30 minutes, but the sky told a different story. She needed to find her way back to the house.

CHAPTER FOUR

It seemed as if she'd been walking through the woods for years because by the time she actually did find her house, her feet were aching terribly. Skie knew the walk couldn't have been that long because she hadn't gotten far in her morning walk. Maybe she was just going in circles for too long in panic.

She walked through the old screen door and tried her flower again.

It replied:

"Wait for the good thing to come to you."

Skie looked at the flower and asked it what it meant by that. The flower had become silent after that line and didn't even lean forward. Skie walked to the couch in the living room and put her feet up. She looked at the time on the Ticking Clock, a name given to the Greek clock by her great uncle, Abram. He actually hated the clock because it ticked too loudly, which made him get it modified to muffle the ticking sound.

She turned the TV on and looked back at the clock which read 5 pm. News about the recent gang shooting flashed violently on TV. Interviews and testimonies from victims and doctors were put on display for people to see as far as neighboring states. Thankfully there were no deaths, just injuries.

Skie was annoyed at the foolish display of people who spoke on behalf of these criminals in their interviews. One of the gang members' father was even allowed, during the news interview, to threaten anyone who testified against his son. Skie thought, "How can there be so much evil in this world and yet no one seems to care as long as it brings up the television ratings?"

As Skie grew more annoyed and agitated, she quickly turned off the television and rolled her eyes thinking "When did it get this bad? Nothing like this has ever really happened in this neighborhood. Criminals in the neighborhood weren't unheard of, but the worse they ever seemed to do was sell drugs on the corners. Never have they tried to do anything this reckless.

That's when Skie realized a, now, dead end to the day. First, her flower said nothing and when it did, the message was hard to understand. Then, there was the gang's shootout. Her walk was interrupted and she saw no reason to go back out and try again. The situation scared her terribly to the point where she considered never going outside again. Exhausted and fed up at all that happened today, Skie glued her eyes back onto the television and fell asleep.

~~~~

Skie awakened to the static of the television. The sun shone through the window, almost burning the drapes.

It was morning again. She stared at the television and listened. People were talking, but their voices were muffled. Then the words "**Technical Difficulties**" made its appearance on the television: another thing that rarely happens.

I can't concentrate if all this stuff is happening and there is no one to stop it or no one to help me through it, Skie thought. She sighed and stared at the TV for a long while before getting annoyed. She got up and went to her whispering flower.

"Speak to me, please! It's all I ask for!" Tears began to run down her face and drop into the flower pot, one drop at a time. Yet the flower said nothing.

Skie gave up and heard her stomach growl. Deciding to go get something at her favorite lunch stop, she began to ride her bike down Brooklyn Avenue, waving to many neighbors she had never seen outside their house before.

Shockingly, Mrs. Mary was outside, beautifully dressed in white and lace, with a big smile on her face. Next door to her, Ms. Katie was happily clipping the thorns off her roses.

Before she knew it, Skie approached the restaurant and lay her bike outside on the sidewalk. The bell chimed as she walked in. Smelling the air of grease and sodas, she sighed. Suddenly, a beautiful woman approached her, clearly a waitress.

"Where would you like to sit, darlin'?" The waitress asked. She had gorgeous red hair and freckles. She seemed peppy and popular, like a cheerleader, considering the fact that she looked young enough to be one.

After choosing a seat by the window, behind a small brick partition, she was given a menu. Another waitress approached her and took her order. Skie ordered her usual lunch of lemonade and grilled cheese sandwiches. The waitress left with a nod and went to go fill a cup up with lemonade.

As she waited, Skie looked out the window at the red and black cars that passed. It seemed as if those were the only colored cars there were other than a few white ones here and there.

Lemonade in hand, the waitress returned, telling Skie her sandwiches will be out in a few minutes. Typical.

As the waitress walked back behind the chefs' doors, a man in all black rushed in with a gun pointing to the ceiling. Everyone got under their dining tables as fast as they could muster. She watched behind the brick wall that separated her from the cash register. The man hopped over the counter to the register. The waitress that was tending to Skie's food was hiding behind the kitchen door, her face still visible in the small window.

"Where's the money?" The masked man asked. The waitress faintly yelled, "It's in the cash register!" The masked man looked around for the voice and then finally told everyone to stand. No one stood. He shot his gun 2 times in the air and the waitress jolted up. The man pointed to her with the gun and said, "Open the register." The waitress nervously moved towards it.

"Please put your gun down, sir. We have no security cameras or security. Please, it would make us feel safer." The man laughed at that last statement. Skie ducked her head as the man rolled his eyes in her direction.

She heard 5 shots that were aimed at her and afterwards heard 2 groans and a scream. At another attempt, he shot 6 times and hit three people.

Skie heard the cash register close. Thinking the gunman had left the diner, Skie thought it a clear sign to get up. So she did. As Skie rose up from under the table, she heard 4 shots aimed at her and one hit her in the middle of her arm. She let out a scream and got back under the table. She looked at the bleeding wound and began to cry quietly. She closed her eyes, and stifled in another scream that was waiting to come out.

After five minutes of aching and bleeding, someone yelled, "He's gone!" Everyone made their way out of the diner and a couple people began calling police. Police cars and emergency trucks sped around the corner towards the diner with sirens blazing. Skie began to flash back to that catastrophic day in her life and immediately wanted to be far away from it so she ran, grabbed her bike and pedaled as fast as she could to the only person who would know what to do, her Grandmother. She approached the door of her Grandmother's house and with tears running down her face began banging quickly at the door, hoping her grandmother was home. Skie was so short of breath, she could only gasp the words "help, grandma, please" as he fell to the ground in front of the door.

Grandma Adeline opened the door expecting to see her granddaughter whom she had been waiting for to visit that day.

"Hey darling! I've been waiting for you all day..."

In a whisper from below, Skie reached up saying, "Grandma, help... I've been shot!"

"Oh NO! What?! Skie... Who did this? SOMEBODY HELP!"

Her Grandmother rushed inside, grabbed her keys, and with all the strength she could muster she lifted Skie off the ground and put her in the car.

"We need to get to the Hospital FAST!" her Grandmother said, interrupting Skie's thoughts.

Skie was scared and confused. She became more and more weakened by the loss of blood from the gunshot wound. Skie eventually fell unconscious remembering the last words of her parents and telling herself, *I guess this is the end.*

CHAPTER FIVE

The last thing Skie remembered was being in her grandmother's car. Skie awakened confused and it hadn't yet dawned on her that it was another day. The Sun in the sky, again, shone brightly through the drapes in the hospital bedroom and the worst of yesterday flooded her mind. She looked around and realized her Grandmother was in a chair right next to her. Skie looked at her arm and saw stitches. Cutting through the silence in the room, she looked at her Grandmother, who had a book in her hand, and asked, "Grandma, what are you reading?"

With a smile and sigh of relief Grandma Adeline replied, "Welcome back, beautiful. You had me worried for a minute. I'm reading an old story that

I used to read to your mother." Skie nodded and smiled. "Oh! Here's my favorite part of the story. It's one of my favorite quotes, "it reads, 'nobody can hurt you more than this world. It is very hard for you to trust people, I understand, but you will have to cope with the world either way it goes. As long as you live, just know that I love you.' A beautiful sentiment isn't it?"

"My mom used to say that all the time. I thought that quote was self-made." Her grandmother shook her head and replied by saying, "No, she got it from this book. Man, did she love this story. Never could she keep her eyes and hands off of it. She must've read it at least 30 times throughout her life."

A nurse walked into the room, interrupting the nice conversation between Skie and her grandmother. "Well hello sleeping beauty. So glad you're awake.

However, you've lost a lot of blood. Luckily for you, there was this nice angel that came by to donate. Maybe you know her." The nurse opened the door wider and in walked in Aunt Alicia.

Skie's eyes immediately filled with tears and a huge smile spread across her face. Skie looked at her grandmother and her aunt and suddenly had an overwhelming feeling of love and hope which quickly masked the pain of her injuries. Not knowing how much she had longed for family closeness, Skie wrapped her arms around her aunt and grandmother and began to cry uncontrollably.

The nurse, then touched Skie's arm and said, "It's time for your medicine." Skie lay back as the nurse drew up some medication in a syringe and pushed it into her I.V. Skie began to feel sleepy and weak again and right before she fell asleep she felt a slight nudge of unrest as if there was more trouble

lingering in the atmosphere.

What could it be? How much more can Skie

endure?

CHAPTER SIX

Skie's aunt sat close by Skie's bedside holding one of her hands. The nurse walked in to reassure them that Skie would be fine since she received the blood transfusion. "She should be waking up soon. She may still have some pain but..." just then, they heard a small sigh and looked over to see Skie waking up.

"Hello Skie. I was just talking to your aunt. Since you're awake, you'll be able to go home soon," the nurse explained.

Skie looked over to her aunt and was revisited by the joy she felt before she went to sleep. She then looked for her grandmother, but didn't see her there.

She began to panic and asked the nurse where she was.

"In the bathroom. Don't worry, she'll be back," said the nurse on her way out. Skie sighed and began to relax.

Her aunt sat at the foot of the bed and waited patiently for her grandmother. After a few minutes of awkwardness, her grandmother strolled into the room and took her rightful place in the chair next to Skie's bed.

Grandma Adeline smiled at Aunt Alicia and asked, "Did I ever read this story to you?" She held up the book in her hand to reveal the title.

"No, I don't remember. But you know I never liked reading or listening. After a while I think you just gave up on trying to make me." her aunt answered with a slight giggle.

Grandma Adeline laughed in return saying, "You are absolutely right about that. You were always running..."

With a gasp, Skie's grandmother sat up and had a very worried look on her face. Her wrinkled hand made her way to her heart slowly as she began taking short breaths. She tried to smile through the pain but Skie knew that something was up. She suddenly remembered that feeling of unrest in the atmosphere she felt earlier.

"What's wrong?" Now it was Skie's turn to be worried.

"My chest hurts," her Grandmother replied.

"Do you need a nurse? I can call one," said Aunt Alicia.

Grandma Adeline replied, "No. It isn't that serious. Just a little heartburn."

Skie brushed the fear off her shoulders and watched as her Grandmother laid back in the chair, gently placing her head back on the head rest.

Skie's worries grew as she said, "You're starting to turn pale. I think we should ring for a nurse."

"No! Its okay you guys. Stop worrying yourselves," replied Grandma Adeline.

"I'm not taking any chances," Skie said.

"Skie and Alicia!" grandma quickly exclaimed.

"Yes?" Skie and her aunt replied at the same time.

In a soft whisper, Grandma Adeline said, "Whatever happens in this crazy world, just know that I love you."

"I love you, too Grandma." Skie reached over the bed to give her grandmother a kiss. Her grandmother closed her eyes, seeming to enjoy the moment. The book she was holding slipped out her weak hands and she took a short breath. One tear slowly fell down Grandma Adeline's face right before she slowly started letting Skie's hand go.

"Grandma? Are you okay?" Skie sat up straight in the hospital bed and began yelling. "Grandma! Grandma! Please answer me! Please don't leave me! Grandma!" Skie's aunt yelled for help as Skie held to her grandmother as tight as she could while crying uncontrollably.

Skie rested her head on her grandmother's chest yelling between sobs, "PLEASE GRANDMA! I NEED YOU! PLEASE DON'T LEAVE!"

I NEED A NURSE NOW! PLEASE HELP!"
her aunt yelled as Skie continued to cry loudly.

Nurses and doctors rushed in and saw Skie's grandmother appearing to be unconscious. They all immediately knew to act quickly as they tried unsuccessfully to awaken her.

One nurse pried Skie from her grandmother as the others lifted her onto a stretcher and rushed her out of the room immediately.

As they carried her Grandmother away in a rush while working to revive her, Skie called after her saying, "It's not over, Grandma. I have faith in you. Don't leave. Please, don't leave." Skie continued to cry as she watched the back of her grandmother's head leave the room. The color of her hair reminded Skie of the angels she had imagined her parents to be. A tear ran down her face and she turned to her window where, to her surprise, she spotted her flower.

"What are you doing here?" Skie rubbed the petals of her bedside friend and her smile widened when it replied. "I could never leave you no matter what may happen."

That was something her mother had said before she died. Although Skie's main instinct said to cry, she couldn't because of what the flower had just whispered to her.

She felt that not only was her mother watching over her, but somehow the flower was watching over her too. The flower, though a simple being found near its own death, had been nurtured and seemed to return the favor. It was always near, offering words of encouragement and support and often times changing the way Skie thought about bad situations.

Skie was overcome with gratefulness and peace of mind. With this new found rest, Skie fell asleep thinking about all the people who cared about her even those who are no longer here on earth.

~~~

"Good morning, Miss Skie and Miss Alicia."

"Good morning nurse," they both replied.

"We need to talk about something."

The nurse moved closer to Skie's bed and put a cup of warm tea in her hand. Skie began to drink as she listened intently awaiting the good news about her grandmother.

The nurse began to explain, "Well, as you know, yesterday, your Grandmother was taken to the ICU after having suffered a heart attack." She paused for a sign that Skie and Aunt Alicia understood what she was saying. "Well, we were able to restart her heart and bring her back but..." Skie smiled widely and with excitement interrupted the nurse asking, "So can I see her?"

The nurse's face suddenly became grim and frowned as she continued on saying, "Unfortunately, after monitoring her overnight and providing the best standard of care, your grandmother's heart stopped beating, once again, and we were not able to revive her the second time... I'm so sorry for your loss." The nurse squeezed Skie's hand as a gesture of sympathy and walked out of the room.

Skie stood still with her eyes wide and her mouth open. She was paralyzed in her thoughts. In a flash, she returned back to the time when her parents died. Tears flowed down her face. She wanted to scream but the sound wouldn't come out of her mouth. She was rushed with feelings of anger and mourning all over again.

Aunt Alicia grabbed hold of Skie as they both fell into each other's arms in tears. Skie's world, once again, became cold and dark.

How will she be able to get through, yet another indescribable loss? Will she find the hope she needs to survive?

CHAPTER SEVEN

After being discharged from the hospital, Skie's aunt helped her into the house and laid her on the couch to stare at the creepy television again.

"I'm going to the store to pick up a few things," her aunt whispered. "Is that okay?"

Skie nodded and watched as the one piece of family she had left walk out the door. She tried hard not to think about what happened in the hospital but it was impossible. She began to cry, the minute she heard the door shut.

She decided to get up and walk to the flower that found itself back in its place on the windowsill. She put her hands around it as if she were praying and she began to smile.

"That's my girl," the flower whispered through its petals. Skie was taken back because it sounded so much like her mother's voice. "Mom?"

"I knew you'd recognize my voice," it whispered. In a subtle burst, a white light covered her like a blanket and her mother seemed to appear rising from one of the flower's petals like a hologram. Skie was brought to tears and her mother's hand reached over to her and gently wiped her tears away.

"Honey, you don't need to cry. I am always with you just like I promised. I've been here the whole time," whispered Skie's mother. She continued on saying, "This world is a scary place, I know. But you, my princess, are a very special soldier and you've been given the power over the wickedness and darkness of this world. Because of that, nothing can hurt you. You have to remember this. Never forget that WE are always here to guide you and protect you."

"Yes baby, like me!" Her Grandmother appeared right next to her mother and gave Skie a kiss on the cheek. Skie began to cry even more.

"Don't forget me!" Her father appeared and chimed in saying, "I love you as well and we are all watching over you."

They all embraced Skie in a magical moment before they seemed to disappear back into the petals of the flower. Just then, Aunt Alicia walked in with bags in her hand talking to herself and looking as though she had seen a ghost. She seemed shocked or maybe even scared.

In an instant with excitement in their voices, they both looked at one another and exclaimed, "You won't believe what just happened to me!"

"I saw mom, dad, and grandma," Skie yelled.

"I saw your parents and grandma," Aunt Alicia yelled.

"What? Who? How?" They both exclaimed in confusion of each other's statements.

"Okay! You go first," Aunt Alicia said.

Skie began to utter random phrases in excitement, "It was magical… there was a white light… we hugged… they told me I'M A SOLDIER! It was great...I'm ok...it was just so…"

"Slow down honey," Aunt Alicia replied. "Wow… they all came to me the same way, in the grocery store, right from a bed of roses. Amazing," Aunt Alicia said in awe of the events.

Aunt Alicia took Skie by the hands and said, "This means that with a simple whisper of a flower, our prayers have been answered and now we know that even though things may seem bad, ALL things work for good in our lives. Now THAT, my princess, makes life worth living and fighting for."

Skie wrapped her arms around her aunt and held on tight to the feeling of peace, love, joy, and hope that now filled her heart.

Sneak Peak:

The Whispering Angels

By Jasmine Garrison

PROLOGUE

One year after the death of Grandma Adeline and the miraculous reunion between Aunt Alicia, Skie, Grandma Adeline, and Skie's parents, both Skie and Aunt Alicia had begun to rebuild their lives and were at the greatest peace they'd been in a long time.

However, Skie's mind was in full gear all the time wondering how? How could she have experienced such a miraculous reunion? What if there are others? How is it possible for the whispering flower to still be alive and just as bright as it had been a year ago? Could this be a phenomenon that others should know about? Could this be a new way of reaching our heavenly loved ones? What does the flower have to do with it? Does this mean they are all angels?

CHAPTER ONE
Preview

Skie awakened to the smell of french vanilla coffee and chicory and apple wood bacon. With a sudden onset of hunger, she got up, washed up quickly, and headed into the kitchen where Aunt Alicia was making breakfast while humming an unfamiliar tune.

"So, what's for breakfast?" asked Skie.

"Your favorite. Blueberry waffles and applewood bacon," replied Aunt Alicia. "Sit down and let's eat."

As Skie began to scuffle down her waffle, she looked over to the windowsill where she caught a small gleam of light coming from her flower. Skie paused and smiled.

"Are you okay?" asked Aunt Alicia.

"Yes. It's a beautiful day," replied Skie. "So, it seems we both have guardian angels in common that like to communicate through flowers. I'm so amazed at how this happened. I wonder…" Skie paused.

"Wonder what honey?" Aunt Alicia asked.

"That maybe this isn't the first instance where an angel has tried to talk to someone they knew here on earth," said Skie.

"What if.." Skie paused again.

"Go on honey," said Aunt Alicia.

"What if there are more?" asked Skie.

"More?" replied Aunt Alicia who was unsure where the conversation was going.

Skie went on, "I don't even think I want to know… but what if there are more angels wanting to communicate with their loved ones? Or what if there are more loved ones wishing to see THEIR angels? Could it be just us or could there be more?"

Stay tuned for book 2 of the series

coming December 2016